BATTRON
THE EVIL EYE

WRITTEN AND ILLUSTRATED BY
WAYNE VANSANT

COPY EDITOR: SUSAN BARROWS

BATTRON: THE EVIL EYE. Graphic Novel. Published by Caliber Comics, a division of Caliber Entertainment LLC. Copyright 2024 Wayne Vansant. All Rights Reserved. No part of this book may be copied or retransmitted without the express written permission of the copyright holder and publisher. Limited use of art may be used for journalistic or review purposes. Any similarities to individuals either living or dead is purely coincidental and unintentional except where fair use laws apply. For more information visit the Caliber Comics website: www.calibercomics.com

BATTRON
THE EVIL EYE

NEWS FROM THE FRONT LINE

JULY, 1943.

IN PREPARATION FOR THE BRITISH-AMERICAN INVASION OF SICILY, BATTRON PARACHUTES ONTO THE ISLAND WITH A MIXED GROUP OF ALLIED INTELLIGENCE OPERATORS. LED BY HIS OLD COMRADE CAPTAIN BRYAN WATSON-COLE (SOE), AND A YOUNG LT. ROBERT BECK (OSS) WHO HAS FAMILY RELATIONS IN THE ITALIAN POPULATION, AND UNDERWORLD CONNECTIONS STRETCHING BACK TO THE NEW YORK MAFIA.

THE TEAM IS ON SICILY TO OBSERVE AND REPORT ON GERMAN TROOP AND SUPPLY MOVEMENTS TO THE FRONT. BUT BY SEEKING THE AID OF THE LOCAL UNDERWORLD, THEY MAY HAVE PUT THEMSELVES UP FOR SALE TO THE GERMANS.

WHEN THE INVASION FINALLY COMES, AND THE WHEELS OF BATTLE BEGIN TO TURN IN EARNEST, BATTRON AND HIS TEAM GO ABOUT THEIR JOB OF PROFESSIONALLY OBSERVING AND REPORTING GERMAN MOVEMENTS DOWN A MAJOR MOUNTAIN ROAD. BUT WHEN ONE OF THEIR TEAM COMMITS A SINGLE INNOCENT DISCRETION, THE WHOLE MISSION IS THROWN INTO TURMOIL, WHICH COULD CAUSE THE DEATH OF HUNDREDS, MAYBE THOUSANDS, AND EVEN HAMPER THE OUTCOME OF THE INVASION.

THE BATTRON ADVENTURES:

BATTRON: THE TROJAN WOMAN
BATTRON: BEFORE THE CHARIOTS
BATTRON: AFTER THE CHARIOTS
BATTRON: THE JETTATURA
BATTRON: THE EVIL EYE

SICILY, SUMMER, 1943. AFTER A GOOD NIGHTS REST, BATTRON'S GROUP IS READY FOR ANOTHER DAY BEHIND GERMAN LINES.
OKAY, I'M ALL RESTED UP AND READY FOR ANOTHER DAY...
WELL, I FEAR IT'S GOING TO BE A BAD ONE. FRANK HASN'T MADE TWO TIME CHECKS AND WE CAN'T GET IN TOUCH. TONY HASN'T CHECKED IN, EITHER.
THINK IT COULD BE AN EQUIPMENT PROBLEM?
NO...FRANK'S TOO GOOD AT HIS JOB FOR THAT TO BE A FACTOR. I THINK IT IS MOST LIKELY GARAFALO--BUT NO MATTER WHAT, WE NEED TO SEE WHAT'S UP.

ALL RIGHT, LET'S GO HAVE A LOOK...
I'LL GO WITH YOU.
SO WILL I!

OH NO, YOU DON'T, CANDELORA....
YOU HAVE A JOB HERE.

NO MOVEMENT...AND I SURE DON'T SEE THAT LAZY PALMIERI...

OH, NO...
FRANK...

WHO IN HELL IS "BILLY PALADINO"?
QUESTO È PER BILLY PALADINO

I'M NOT SURPRISED HIS RADIO'S SMASHED.
SO... WHO IS THIS PALADINO?

I'M AFRAID I'LL HAVE TO ANSWER THAT. IT GOES BACK QUITE A WAYS...
YOU SEE, I KILLED HIM.

"MY UNCLE GIOSEPA HAD SURVIVED AS A SMALL-TIME INDEPENDENT OPERATOR WHO RAN A FEW LUCRATIVE RACKETS. SOME OF THEM WERE HOTLY COVETED BY SEVERAL AMBITIOUS LOCAL THUGS.
"IN THE FALL OF 1941, THREE OF THE TOUGHS CAUGHT MY UNCLE IN A DARK ALLEY...

"AND...

"HIS DEATH HIT MY MOTHER THE HARDEST. SHE WEPT BITTER TEARS FOR THE OLDER BROTHER WHOM SHE HAD LOVED SO VERY MUCH.

"AS FOR ME, I DEALT WITH IT IN A WHOLLY DIFFERENT WAY...
"I SWORE VENGEANCE!

"OVER THE COURSE OF THE NEXT THREE MONTHS, I SCOURED THE GRIMY BELLY OF THE UNDERWORLD, SEEKING TO DIG UP ANY AND ALL CLUES ON WHO HAD COMMITTED THIS OUTRAGE.

"I FINALLY CAME ACROSS ONE NAME--THAT OF BILLY PALADINO.

"IN JANUARY 1942, I TRACKED HIM TO EDISON, NEW JERSEY. WHEN HE CAME STUMBLING DRUNK OUT OF A BAR...

"...I DEALT WITH THAT BASTARD THE SAME WAY HE AND HIS LOUSY PARTNERS DEALT WITH MY UNCLE.
"AND THAT'S THE STORY OF BILLY PALADINO."

C'MON, GET YOUR MINDS OFF VENGEANCE.
KEEP THEM ON THE JOB AT HAND.

TONY, FRANK IS DEAD AND HIS RADIO'S SMASHED. IT WAS GARAFALO'S MEN THAT DID IT.
RADIO WATSON-COLE TO LET HIM KNOW.

WE GOT MORE GOING ON HERE... WE SPOTTED SOME OF GARAFALO'S MEN ON THEIR WAY UP HERE.

SOMETHING'S HAPPENING IN RANDAZZO--A LOT OF VEHICLES LOOKING HEAVILY LADEN ARE BEING HIDDEN UNDER THE TREES.

WE'LL COME FROM UP ABOVE, SO WE CAN SEE GARAFALO'S MEN BEFORE THEY CAN SPOT US.

OKAY. TELL THAT TO WATSON-COLE. WE'LL BE RIGHT UP...

ANOTHER HARD DAY...

SOON...

EVERYBODY ALL RIGHT?
YEAH! WE WERE READY FOR THEM.

OKAY, PACK UP THE RADIO AND EVERYTHING YOU NEED, AND LET'S GET OUTTA--
BAT, WE'VE ALREADY DONE THAT..
BUT FIRST, I GOT TO SHOW YOU SOMETHING.

UNDER EVERY TREE ON THE WEST AND SOUTH SIDE OF RANDAZZO IS A HIDDEN TRUCK, COVERED WITH CAMOUFLAGE NETTING AND TREE LIMBS...
WHAT DO YOU THINK IT MEANS, TONY?

NO TELLING WHAT THEY'VE GOT HIDDEN IN TOWN. I KNOW WHAT THIS MEANS...
THEY'RE PLANNING ON RUNNING A CONVOY DOWN THAT ROAD...TONIGHT.

YOU REALLY THINK SO?
MUST BE! WE NEED TO PULL BACK ACROSS THE ROAD AND SET UP AT A SAFE SPOT.
GET IN TOUCH WITH WATSON-COLE AND HAVE HIM PASS THIS INFO ON TO THE BOMBER BOYS.

ONCE THAT HAPPENS, WE'LL HAVE TO BUG OUT! THE ITALIANS AND GERMANS WILL SWARM THESE HILLS LOOKING FOR WHO'S RESPONSIBLE.

BECK, FIND A GOOD PLACE TO CALL WATSON-COLE. HIDE WELL, BUT WATCH FOR US SO WE CAN FIND YOU. WE'LL KEEP IN TOUCH ON THE HANDIE-TALKIES.
WILL DO, BAT!

ALL RIGHT, LADIES-- LOOKS LIKE WE WILL HAVE TO ABANDON THIS POST SOON...
...LIKELY BY TOMORROW MORNING. YOU THREE HAVE THE JOB OF GATHERING AS MUCH FOOD AS WE CAN CARRY.
NOTHING FANCY-- BREAD, WINE, FRUIT, ANYTHING WE DON'T HAVE TO COOK...

I HAVE SOME GOOD HARD SAUSAGE WE COULD CARRY, AND PLENTY OF IT.
THAT SOUNDS GREAT.

WE'LL BE GOING IN THE TRUCK AS FAR AS WE CAN, BUT WE MAY BE FORCED TO WALK...
PACK WHATEVER MAKES THE MOST SENSE TO YOU.

THESE PANTS I'M WEARING ARE TOO BIG AND GETTING WORN OUT--AND SO ARE MY SANDALS.
I'M SURE TO HAVE SOMETHING SHE CAN WEAR.
NOTHING TOO COLORFUL!

DO YOU HAVE ANYTHING LIKE A HEAVY SKIRT?
I'M SURE I DO. LET'S GO SHOPPING!

LOT OF ACTIVITY IN THERE...
WHAT IS THAT ON THE SIDE STREET?

THAT, MY FRIEND, IS A TIGER TANK! THEY DON'T USUALLY TRAVEL ALONE.

LET'S SLIP OUTTA HERE.

ANDRU, I WAS WONDERING ABOUT THAT COMMENT GARAFALO MADE THE FIRST DAY AT THE BIG HOUSE ABOUT NAPLES...
I WAS AFRAID THAT WOULD COME UP AGAIN.

YEARS AGO, HE HIRED ME TO TEND SOME CATTLE HE HAD UP IN THESE SAME HILLS. BUT I DIDN'T KNOW THEY WERE STOLEN!
WHEN THE POLICE NABBED ME WITH THEM, HE DENIED ANY KNOWLEDGE. I SPENT 18 MONTHS IN PRISON SIMPLY FOR TENDING THAT CROOK'S DAMNED CATTLE!

LATER THAT AFTERNOON, BATTRON'S GROUP FOUND BECK AND HIS GROUP ON A HIGH PEAK WITH A GREAT VIEW.
WE'RE CLOSE ENOUGH HERE TO GET WATSON-COLE ON THE HANDIE-TALKIE.
HELL, THIS VANTAGE POINT IS BETTER THAN ANYTHING GARAFALO SHOWED US.

WE'RE IN A REALLY GOOD SPOT UP HERE. THE ROAD FROM RANDAZZO IS VISIBLE FOR MILES TO THE WEST, ALMOST TO THE FAR END.

OUR HANDLERS ARE EXCITED ABOUT THIS, BUT THEY'LL NEED OUR HELP TO HIT THE TARGET IN THE DARK.

I'VE GOT TO GO MEET WATSON-COLE. HE HAS A COUPLE OF FLARE PISTOLS WE MIGHT NEED. WE'RE GOING TO BE RUNNING OUR ASSES OFF TONIGHT.
WELL, AS YOU SAID EARLIER, ANOTHER HARD DAY...
...AND A HARD NIGHT.

OKAY, LET'S GET THE RADIO EQUIPMENT READY...
THAT WAY WE CAN BREAK IT DOWN IN A HURRY WHEN THE TIME COMES.
I'LL TAKE CARE OF THAT, CAPTAIN.

CAPTAIN WATSON-COLE, I THINK YOU COULD MAKE BETTER USE OF ME IN AN OUTSIDE JOB.
IS THAT RIGHT, CARLO?

BELIEVE ME, I AM WORTHY OF YOUR TRUST. YOU HAVE NOTHING TO LOSE.
BUT YOU DO IF YOU BETRAY US, I'LL GET BATTRON TO TAKE YOU OUT BACK AND CUT YOUR THROAT.

WELL, CANDELORA! I SEE YOU GOT A CHANGE OF CLOTHES.
YES, THIS IS BETTER TO RUN FIGHT IN. BUT I COULD NOT FIND ANY SHOES TO FIT ME.

BUT I DID FIND THESE WOOL SOCKS, WHICH ARE GOOD AND THICK. HOWEVER...
THEY DON'T MATCH.

WE HAVE A PILE OF UNIFORM TUNICS IN THE BACK OF THE TRUCK. COULD YOU GET THEM?
CERTAINLY, CAPTAIN WATSON-COLE.

I HAVE MY OWN UNIFORM, CAPTAIN.

BUONA SERATA, BAT.
BONNE APRES-MIDI, CANDELORA.
COULD I HELP YOU WITH THAT?

DO WE NEED THE CAPS?
YES, WE NEED THE CAPS.

OKAY, BAT...I WANT BECK AND YOU IN GERMAN UNIFORMS, AND ANDRU IN ITALIAN. CARLO WILL GO WITH ANDRU. I JUST HOPE THAT WE CAN TRUST HIM.

TELL ANDRU TO GET BACK HERE QUICK. IT'S LATE IN THE DAY.

WHEN THE FIREWORKS START, PUT SOME DISTANCE BETWEEN YOU AND THE ROAD, OKAY?

BATTRON ISSUED EVERYONE THEIR ASSIGNMENTS.
OKAY, SO WE KNOW WHAT WE GOT TO DO. LET'S GET TO IT.

TONY, YOU STICK WITH THE RADIO. BE READY TO BREAK IT DOWN WHEN THE TIME COMES.

ANDRU, YOU'LL GO WITH CARLO. I THINK HE CAN BE TRUSTED, BUT...WATCH YOUR BACK.

THE LAST SUNLIGHT OF THE DAY SHONE ON A LONE MOSQUITO THAT WAS CIRCLING OVERHEAD, AWAITING INSTRUCTION FROM WATSON-COLE'S GROUP.

GOOD LUCK, ANDRU. KEEP WATCH ON YOU KNOW WHO.

IT WILL BE DARK SOON. HOW FAR OFF IS WHERE WE ARE GOING?
DON'T WORRY. I'VE BEEN UP AND DOWN THESE MOUNTAINS ENOUGH TO KNOW EXACTLY WHERE WE'RE HEADED.

WHAT'S THAT?
IT'S THE POLICE MOTOR-TRICYCLE THAT ROBERTO AND I HID.

THERE'S THE ROAD. NOW, WE START TO PICK UP STICKS AND BRANCHES.

LET'S MAKE THIS A LITTLE BIGGER-- EASY FOR THE BOMBERS TO SEE, AND FOR US TO HIT WITH THE VERY-LIGHT.
SOUNDS GOOD TO ME.

HOW DID YOU GET INTO THIS CRAZY WORK, BOB? IS IT A LONG STORY?
NOT LONG AT ALL.

"THE FIRST THING MY DAD DID WHEN HE HEARD THE NEWS OF PEARL HARBOR WAS TO RUN TO THE TRAIN STATION.
New York World-Telegram
1500 DEAD IN HAWAII
CONGRESS VOTES WAR

"HE TOOK THE FIRST TRAIN TO WASHINGTON TO CONSULT WITH HIS OLD FRIEND...

"...NOW GENERAL "WILD BILL" DONOVAN, HEAD OF THE NEWLY FORMED OFFICE OF STRATEGIC SERVICES.
MY SON IS A SMART YOUNG MAN, SPEAKS VERY GOOD GERMAN AND ITALIAN...
THOUGH AT TIMES HE CAN BE HEADSTRONG, GOING HIS OWN WAY...

"ACTUALLY, I THOUGHT IT WAS A GREAT IDEA. I JOINED ENTHUSIASTICALLY.
"I WAS SHIPPED OFF TO BETHESDA, MARYLAND, TO GO THROUGH MY OSS TRAINING. TRAINERS NOTICED HOW EXPERIENCED I ALREADY WAS WITH THE PISTOL AND THE KNIFE.

"THEN, I WAS INTRODUCED TO A VARIETY OF THE ITALIAN DIASPORA--OLD ROYALTY, CHRISTIAN DEMOCRATS, FORMER FASCISTS, COMMUNISTS--WHO WERE PROVIDING VITAL INTELLIGENCE TO BENEFIT OUR ITALIAN SECTION.

SOUNDS LIKE YOUR FATHER STEERED YOU IN THE RIGHT PATH.
YES, HE DID--IN MORE WAYS THAN HE WOULD EVER KNOW.

I'D LIVED IN THE MIDDLE OF DIFFERENT SOCIETIES ALL MY LIFE, AND LEARNED TO ENJOY IT. I'M A NATURAL SPY!

THIS LOOKS GOOD. EASY TO HIT THE BRUSHPILE WITH THE FLARE GUN, AND IT'LL BE FAR ENOUGH OFF THE ROAD WHEN ALL THE FIREWORKS BEGIN.
I'LL TAKE THE FIRST WATCH. WHY DON'T YOU TAKE A NAP...

LET'S GET MOVING.
I'LL CUT IN MIDWAY
DOWN THE COLUMN.

I SEE 'EM!

LET'S SEE IF I CAN HIT IT...

...BINGO!

THERE IT IS!

HERE WE GO!

NO, I HAVE NEVER BEEN TO GENOA...

IN FACT, THE ONLY TIME I HAVE BEEN OFF THE ISLAND OF SICILY WAS WHEN I WAS THROWN INTO THE JAIL IN NAPLES.

I CAN SEE NOTHING GOOD ABOUT TRAVEL OR POLITICS OR HISTORY.

OKAY...
LET'S PULL IN HERE.

THE CONVOY MOVED ALONG AT ABOUT 10 MILES AN HOUR...

...ILLUMINATING THE ROAD WITH THEIR HOODED HEADLIGHTS.

THE DRIVERS WERE SO INTENT ON WATCHING THE ROAD, THAT THEY FAILED TO SEE BATTRON'S FLARE.

I SEE THE
FIRST FIRE.

I HEAR
THE PLANE.

WHAT
DO WE DO WHEN
THE BOMBERS
GET HERE?

WE HIT THE ROAD.
MAKE AS MUCH DIS-
TANCE AS WE CAN.

THERE
ARE THE
TRUCKS!

WHAT IN HELL?

THERE IS THE SECOND FIRE. LET'S LIGHT UP THE NIGHT!
THE MOSQUITO BEGAN TO DROP BUNCHES OF MULTI-COLORED FALAINS--TARGET INDICATORS.

CHILDREN OF WAR-STRUCK GERMAN CITIES ALREADY HAD A NAME FOR THESE...
...THEY HAD BEGUN CALLING THEM "CHRISTMAS TREES IN THE SKIES."

LET'S GET HIGHER UP!

FROM THE SOUTHWEST, A LONG LINE OF AVRO LANDCASTERS APPEARED.

I DIDN'T THINK IT WOULD BE SO BIG...
COME ON!

BATTRON AND BECK WERE WAY UP THE HILL, BUT FELT THE BLAST STRONGLY.
JEEZ!

ANDRU AND CARLO WERE MUCH CLOSER, SO THEY GOT THE FULL EFFECT.
OOFGHH!

TONY, WE'LL BE THERE AS QUICK AS WE CAN. GET EVERYONE READY TO MOVE.

MEIN GOTT!

UNREIN, GET OFF THE ROAD!

THREE TIGER TANKS BOUND FOR THE HERMAN GORING DIVISION WERE CAUGHT IN THE BOMBING...
TWO TANKS WERE SMASHED.
THE THIRD TIGER TANK PULLED OVER ONTO NARROW TRACK AND CONTINUED ITS PUSH TO THE WEST.

DIEU AU PARADIS...!
DAMN, WE SURE MURDERED THAT BUNCH.
WELL, THAT'S WHAT WE'RE HERE FOR.

HERR, WIE IST DAS PASSIERT...
CAPTAIN ESSENBECK!

I FOUND A HALF TRACK WITH A WORKING DORA RADIO. WHAT DO I DO NOW?
GET IN TOUCH WITH COLONEL LIVORNA...

HE HAS A WHOLE PLATOON OF "GIOVANI FASCISTI" THAT HE'S HELD ONTO. WE NEED THEM. ALSO, GET A FEW MEN AND GO UP AND DOWN THE COLUMN.

FIND ANY MEN WHO ARE FIT TO FIGHT AND STILL HAVE THEIR WEAPONS.
WHAT THEN, CAPTAIN?
THEN, WE SURGE INTO THESE HILLS TO SEEK OUT THE SWINE RESPONSIBLE FOR THIS FIASCO.

AND WHEN WE FIND THEM... WE'LL FLAY THEM ALIVE!

WE'RE OKAY IF WE CAN GET HIGHER UP!
BUONO IN PARADISO, CHE COS'E?
BBRRREEEEEEEEEEH...
...BA-RAM!

IT'S A TIGER TANK, BUT WE'RE OKAY...

IT CAN'T ELEVATE ANY FARTHER UP.

LET'S GET OUT OF HERE AND FIND THE OTHERS.

GLIUPATRA, HOW MANY MEN DO YOU THINK GARAFALO HAS?

I KNOW WE'VE KILLED SEVEN, BUT HOW MANY MORE MIGHT WE ENCOUNTER?
LET'S SEE... I DON'T THINK I'VE SEEN ANY MORE THAN THAT AT ONE TIME.

HE HAS SOME THAT ARE NOT AROUND SO MUCH WHO WORK IN OTHER TOWNS.

HE SOMETIMES BORROWS MEN FROM OTHER DONS FOR SPECIAL NEEDS.

WELL, LET'S HOPE WE DON'T RUN INTO ANY OF THEM.

OKAY, THIS IS WHERE WE HAVE TO CLIMB UP HIGHER INTO THESE HILLS.
BEFORE WE TURN WEST, WE CAN SPREAD OUT A LITTLE, BUT BE SURE TO STAY WITHIN SIGHT OF THOSE WHO ARE IN FRONT AND BEHIND YOU.

BECK, YOU TAKE TO THE REAR, AND KEEP WATCH FOR ANY DANGER BEHIND US...

TONY, ONCE WE CAN REACH WATSON-COLE ON THE HANDIE-TALKIE, WE'LL DUMP OUT THE SCR-284.
THAT SOUNDS GOOD TO ME.

UNREIN HAS GOT EVERY MAN AT THE HEAD OF THE COLUMN. THEY ARE HEADING STRAIGHT UP INTO THE HILLS FROM THERE...
WHAT ABOUT COLONEL LIVORNA'S MEN?

THEY WILL MARCH STRAIGHT WEST FROM RANDAZZO ALONG THE HIGHER SOUTHERN PEAKS.

WE WILL HEAD STRAIGHT NORTH, UP THE HILLS.

AND DURING THE DAYLIGHT HOURS, WE'LL HAVE HIS EYES ABOVE US.

THAT WAS GOOD! WE ALL SEEM TO KNOW WHAT TO DO. EVERYBODY, KEEP YOUR EYES OPEN.

THEY'LL PROBABLY TAKE US RIGHT BY HERE IN THE TRUCK.
OR GO DOWN THE OLD CREEK TRAIL.

DON GARAFALO! WE HAVE A VISITOR. A VERY IMPORTANT VISITOR...!

DON GARAFALO, YOUR OBSESSION WITH THIS "WOMAN" HAS PUT ALL OUR ORGANIZATIONS IN JEOPARDY.

THE AMERICANS HAVE OFFERED US A PRICELESS OPPORTUNITY...
ONE THAT INVOLVES VERY LITTLE WORK AND COST ON OUR PART.

YOUR SELFISH BEHAVIOR COULD HAVE PUT THIS WHOLE OPPORTUNITY IN PERIL.
I'M AFRAID I MUST STEP IN TO REDRESS THE SITUATION.

MIO DIO!

THIS BUNCH IS AFTER US DIRECTLY!

I'LL SEE IF I CAN REACH WATSON-COLE ABOUT THIS!

KEEP YOUR EYES PEELED.

EH? WHY DO I HAVE TO PEEL MY EYES?

JUST AN EXPRESSION. LOOK FOR GERMANS OR ITALIANS OR GARAFALO.

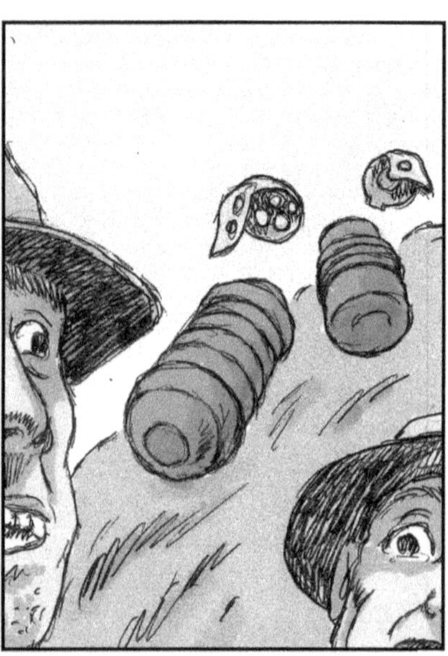

YEAAAH!

THAT CERTAINLY WORKED OUT VERY WELL!

DO YOU THINK WE'LL NEED THAT THING AGAIN?
PROBABLY NOT. BUT, LET'S REMEMBER WHERE IT IS...JUST IN CASE.

WE'RE NOT QUITE READY FOR A REUNION, BOB...

WE'VE GOT MORE WORK TO DO UP THERE.

THESE AMERICANS HAVE PROVIDED US WITH A MOST UNIQUE OPPORTUNITY--A CHANCE TO ERASE WHAT MUSSOLINI DID TO OUR SOCIETY BACK IN THE 1920s...

THIS GROUP CANNOT, MUST NOT BE ALLOWED TO RE-ENTER ALLIED LINES. THEY MUST ALL BE ELIMINATED.
IF EVEN ONE OF THEM GETS AWAY TO REPEAT HIS STORY...

...IT WILL BE YOU WHO MUST EXIT THE SCENE.

CAPTAIN, A GROUP OF ABOUT A DOZEN GERMANS IS HEADING YOUR WAY, MOVING PARALLEL TO THE ONES CHASING US.
I THINK YOU SHOULD TRY AND GET PAST GARAFALO'S PLACE BEFORE THEY REACH YOU.

WE MADE IT! LET'S GIVE WATSON-COLE A CALL.

WE'RE UP ABOVE GARAFALO'S. I SEE A FEW GERMANS COMING UP THE ROAD.

CAN YOU BRING BOTH GROUPS UNDER FIRE?

CARLO AND I CAN HOLD BACK THE GERMANS.

OKAY, LET'S SPRAY THE GERMANS...

...AND THEN HIT THE MAFIA!

WHERE IS THAT COMING FROM?
FROM UP ON THE HILL, I THINK.

ABOVE THEM IN THE HILLS, ESSENBECK'S GROUP COULD HEAR THE GUNFIRE.

I'M GOING TO CRAWL OUT THERE AND GET ME ONE OF THEIR MACHINE PISTOLS.

WE GOT THEIR HEADS DOWN. COME ON.

WE'RE ON OUR WAY!

≿GNAAGH!!!≾

DON GARAFALO! WHAT ARE YOU DOING?

I'M TELLING YOU, THIS IS MOST ILL ADVISED...!

WHAT IN HELL?!

I PROMISE YOU THAT IF YOU CONTINUE ON THIS PATH...

COME ON! SOMETHING'S HAPPENING UP AHEAD!

YOU IDIOT!

LET'S GO FIND TONY AND HIS GROUP.

THAT WAS EASY--THERE THEY ARE! I SEE YOU GOT RID OF THE BIG RADIO.
IT SLOWED US DOWN, SO WE HAD TO DITCH IT.

WE FOUND A GOOD DRY PLACE TO BURY IT. AND WE BURIED THE CRYSTALS-- IN SEPARATE PLACES.

WE HAD TO MOVE FAST TO OUTRUN THEM!

MERDE! ITALIANS FROM RANDAZZO.
LET'S GET MOVING!

OKAY, WE'LL COMBINE MY MEN WITH WHAT YOU HAVE LEFT AND GO AFTER THEM.

WILL WE BE BRINGING HER BACK?
I'M GLAD YOU ASKED THAT.

UNLESS WE CATCH THEM BEFORE THEY CAN REPORT WHAT YOU HAVE BEEN DOING...

...IT IS YOU THAT WE WON'T BE BRINGING BACK.

SOMETHING STRANGE IS GOING ON HERE...IT SEEMS A BLOOD-FEUD HAS ERUPTED AMONG MEMBERS OF THE LOCAL MAFIA!

THAT CAR BELONGS TO A CERTAIN DON GARAFALO--
--BUT THE BULLETHOLES ARE FROM AN MP-40.

WE WERE INFORMED THAT THE LOCAL UNDERWORLD WAS COOPERATING WITH THE AMERICANS. I GUESS THIS PROVES IT.

WE FOUND THIS POLICE TRI-MOTOR CYCLE. IT HAD BLOOD ON IT. WE MIGHT CAN MAKE USE OF IT.

WELL--WHATEVER MAY COME, I WANT TO GET MY HANDS ON THIS BUNCH. THEY HAVE COST US DEARLY.

OKAY...EVERYBODY OUT, BOYS AND GIRLS--WE'RE OUTTA GAS. OR, SOMETHING ABOUT THIS OLD GIRL HAS SAID NO MORE.

LET'S GET RID OF THE BIG RADIO. HOPEFULLY WE CAN REACH BATTRON AND THE OTHERS WITH THE HANDIE-TALKIES.
YES, SIR.

WE'LL TAKE WHAT WE CAN OF THE FOOD IN THESE BAGS.

NOW, LADIES AND GENTLEMEN, LET'S TRY TO GET BACK TO OUR LINES AS QUIETLY AND QUICKLY AS WE CAN.

THEY WERE CONSTANTLY SCANNING THEIR SURROUNDINGS FOR ITALIAN OR GERMAN SOLDIERS.

BUT, THEY ALSO LOOKED ABOVE...

..WATCHING FOR THE EVER-PRESENT STORCH OBSERVATION PLANE THAT WAS LOOKING FOR THEM--

--AND THEM ALONE.

THIS IS GETTING VERY TIRESOME...

SORRY WE GOT YOU MIXED UP IN THIS, MARCU.

THAT'S OKAY. I AM HAVING A REAL ADVENTURE!

HEY, BAT!

I SEE SOME VERY FRIENDLY FACES.

WELL, LOOK WHO'S HERE!
I TOLD YOU WE WOULD GET BACK TOGETHER.

WE GOT A GOOD VIEW OF THE ROAD. IT STILL HAS GERMANS MOVING ALONG IT.
THAT'S NOT OUR JOB, NOW. WE'VE DONE OUR BIT.

NOW, WE'RE JUST SAVING OUR ASS.
RIGHT-O! AND WE'RE CLOSE TO THAT.

WE'VE GOT TO GET OVER THOSE TWO RIDGE MASSES TO REACH THE FLAT VALLEY BEYOND.

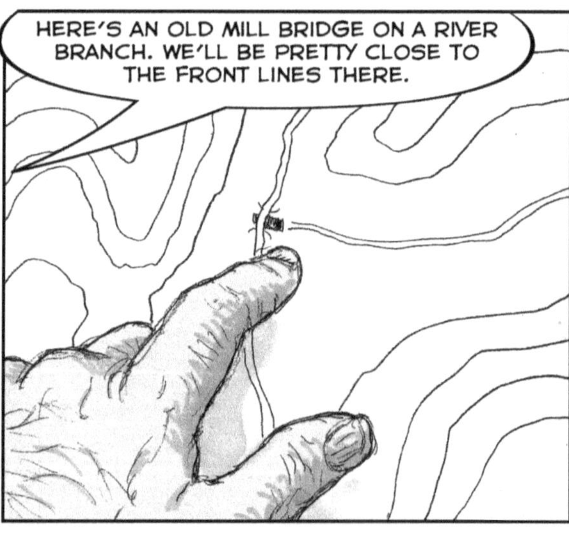

HERE'S AN OLD MILL BRIDGE ON A RIVER BRANCH. WE'LL BE PRETTY CLOSE TO THE FRONT LINES THERE.

...AND THERE'S THE REST OF 'EM!
YOU MAKE TOO MUCH NOISE.
AH, YES! THANKS, I WAS STARVING!
EAT ALL YOU WANT, AND WE WON'T HAVE TO CARRY IT.
WHO ARE YOU CALLING?
I'M LISTENING FOR ANY ALLIED CHATTER...BUT NO JOY.

MAYBE WE SHOULD HAVE KEPT ONE OF THE SCR284S.

TOO HEAVY. WE NEED TO KEEP LIGHT AND QUICK NOW.
AGREED.

THIS IS A GOOD PLACE TO REST--IT'LL BE DARK SOON. WE'LL GET UP AT THE CRACK OF DAWN AND MOVE ON.

FIND A GOOD SPOT IN PAIRS...BUT KEEP ONE EYE OPEN, AND HAVE YOUR WEAPONS AT THE READY.

WELL. I'LL SAY! THAT CERTAINLY DOES MY HEART GOOD!
MAYBE SO...
BUT, THE CLOSER WE COME TO GETTING OUTTA THESE HILLS...

...THE EASIER IT BECOMES FOR THEM TO FIND US.

BAT'S RIGHT! LET'S NOT GET COMPLACENT. KEEP YOUR EYES PEELED.
HOW DO I PEEL MY EYES?

I CAN SEE FOUR OF THEM...BUT WHERE ARE THE REST?

THEY'RE MOVING THROUGH HEAVY BRUSH TO AVOID US SPOTTING THEM.

I'D BETTER GET BACK AND REPORT TO CAPTAIN ESSENBECK!

IT'S AN OLD WINE PRESS AND CANNERY.
WE SHOULD LEAVE SOME MEN HERE, SINCE THEY'RE SURE TO PASS.

WON'T THAT SPREAD US A LITTLE THIN?
THEY'LL WANT TO CHECK IT OUT.

WATCH FOR A CHANCE. THEY'LL WANT TO EXPLORE ANY SHELTER, AND YOU CAN AMBUSH THEM.

WHAT A GANG OF MORONS! I'D BE SAFER BACK IN BROWNSVILLE.

CAPTAIN ESSENBECK!
I JUST SAW FOUR OF THEM!

THEY'RE MOVING THROUGH SOME HEAVY BRUSH.
WE HAVE LOST CONTACT WITH COLONEL LIVORNA--AND NOW IT SEEMS THEY'RE MOVING TOO FAR NORTH.

ARE THEY ALL TOGETHER, OR ARE THEY MOVING IN SEVERAL GROUPS?

IF THEY HAVE OBSERVERS IN THAT BUILDING, THEY WILL EASILY BE ABLE TO SPOT US CROSSING THIS OPEN GROUND...

BUT WE HAVE THE FIREPOWER TO TAKE THEM OUT--IF WE CAN GET IN CLOSER.

THE LEAVES AND GRASS ARE VERY DRY...

...PERFECT FOR MAKING A SMOKESCREEN!

WHAT THE HELL ARE THEY TRYING TO PULL NOW?
THEY KNOW WHAT THEY'RE DOING.

KEEP GOING IN LOW.
THEY WON'T BE ABLE TO SEE US.

AH, HERE'S A NICE, CONVENIENT ENTRANCE...

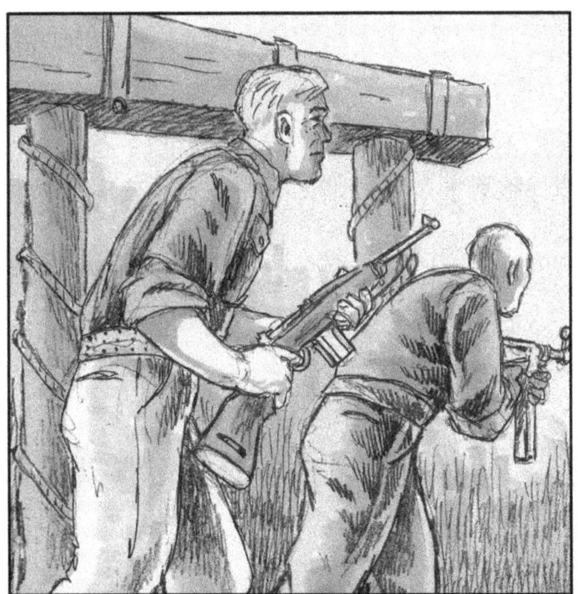

KLANG!
KLANG!
KLANG!
KLANG!
KLANG!

WHAT IS
THAT?

WHAT'S GOING ON OVER
THERE? IT LOOKS LIKE
AN AMBUSH!
LET'S PULL
OVER AND SEE.

BUT, SUDDENLY FROM THEIR LEFT...!

WHO'S HUNTING WHO?
THIS GANG IS NOT VERY SMART.

LET'S GET BACK TO THE OTHERS BEFORE THE SMOKE CLEARS.
GIVE ME A MINUTE...

YOU KNEW WHO I WAS FROM THE BEGINNING, DIDN'T YOU?
YEAH. I SAW YOU WITH BILLY PALADINO ONE TIME.

DOM RAO IS WORKING IN NAPLES WITH VITO GENOVESE. YOU MIGHT GET THERE, IF YOU'RE LUCKY.

BUT, I DOUBT...
...THAT YOU CAN MAKE IT BACK TO PATERSON.

WELL, MAYBE NOT. BUT ONE THING'S FOR SURE.
YOU WON'T GET BACK TO BROWNSVILLE.

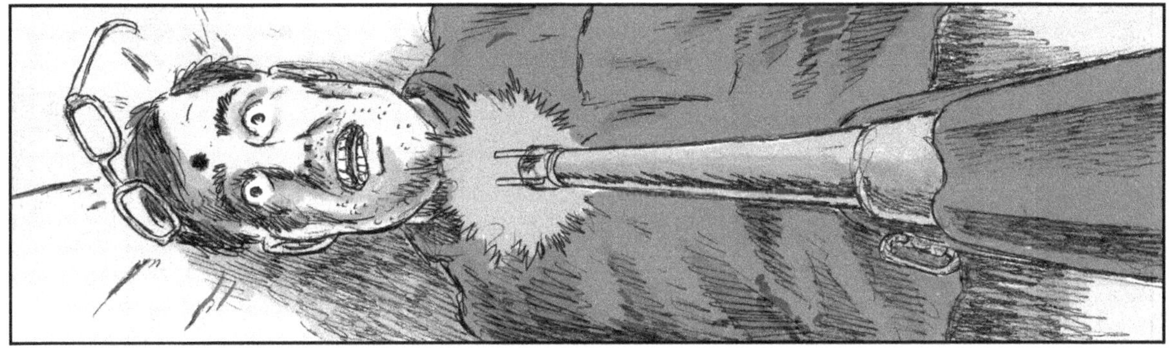

LET'S MOVE.
SEE IF YOU CAN MAKE CONTACT WITH ANY OF OUR UNITS COMING OVER THOSE HILLS.
AW, NO! ALL OUR BATTERIES ARE DEAD!

WE SHOULDN'T GET TOO FAR AHEAD OF CAPTAIN ESSENBECK.
WE NEED MORE BACKUP.

EH!
PROBLEM SOLVED.

IT'D BE EASIER TO SPOT IT FROM UP HERE--THAT IS, IF YOU'D GET OFF THE TRAIL FOR ONCE, BECK!
WHUFF!

YOU ALL RIGHT, BOB?
I'M LAZY! THAT'S WHY I'M IN INTELLIGENCE, NOT THE INFANTRY.

DAMNATION! OUR WATER'S ALL GONE...
AND IF WE FIND A STREAM, THIS THING'S GOT TOO MANY HOLES IN IT TO REFILL.

WE'VE LOST FOUR MORE MEN, AND WE'RE NO CLOSER TO CATCHING UP WITH THEM.

I JUST WANT TO GET THE WOMAN BACK.

WE ARE SEARCHING FOR A GROUP OF ENEMY ALLIED AGENTS.
PERHAPS ABOUT TEN OF THEM.
WHAT WERE THEY DOING BEHIND OUR LINES?

THEY DIRECTED THOSE BOMBERS THAT ATTACKED OUR CONVOY.
SO, WHEN WE RUN THIS SCUM TO GROUND...

...I SHALL BE HONORED TO GRIND THEM TO BLOODY DUST BENEATH MY TREADS.

GOOD MAN! GOOD MAN! LET'S GO GET THEM.

PROBABLY A GRAIN MILL.

THEY HAVE TO COME THROUGH HERE...

LET'S GET AHEAD OF 'EM.
WILL DO.

DAMN! IT'S TOO NARROW FOR US...
YOU IDIOT!
IT'S BUILT FOR FARMERS' CARTS!

OH, LOOK...
WE'VE GOT HELP.

LET'S GET THEIR ATTENTION.

NO! NO! DON'T SHOOT!

I AM NOT YOUR ENEMY!

THE ENEMY OF MY ENEMY IS MY FRIEND!

I'M YOUR FRIEND! NOT YOUR ENEMY!
I'M--

--MMMUUUMMG-GGH!

ON THE SLOPE ABOVE THE MILL...
...WAS A RANGER NAMED JOHNNY RILEY.

JOHNNY RILEY FIRED HIS BAZOOKA...

...AND JOHNNY RILEY WAS ONE HELLUVA GOOD SHOT.

THEN A HAILSTORM OF RANGER MORTARS RAINED DOWN ON THE GERMAN TROOPS.

THE CREW OF THE TIGER, IMMOBILIZED AND UNABLE TO RAISE THEIR GUNS, HAD LITTLE CHOICE BUT TO ABANDON THEIR VEHICLE.

YOU ROTTEN...

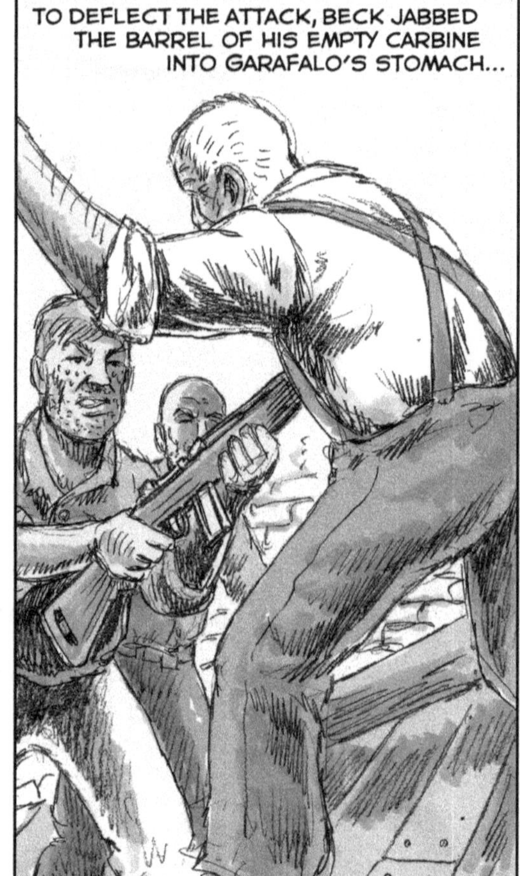

TO DEFLECT THE ATTACK, BECK JABBED THE BARREL OF HIS EMPTY CARBINE INTO GARAFALO'S STOMACH...

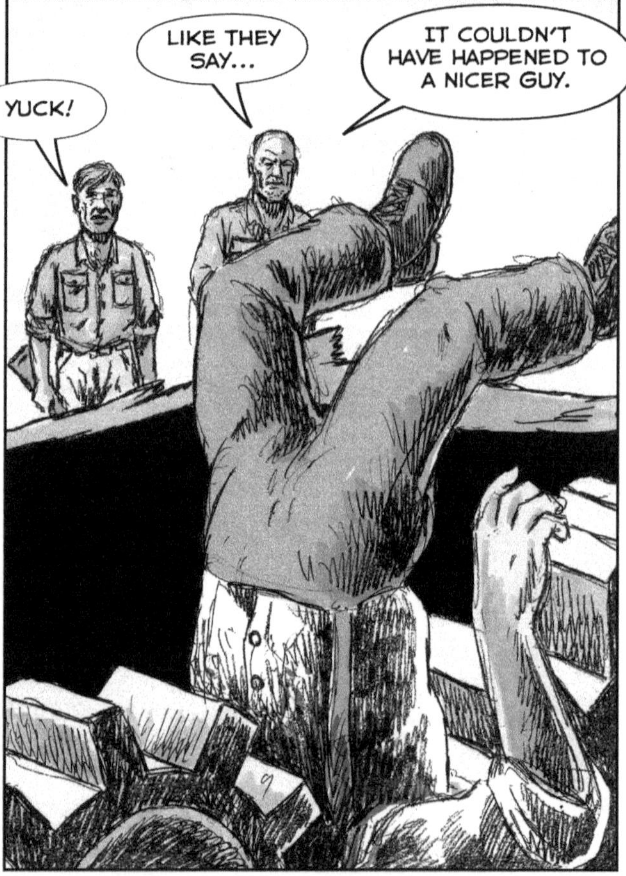

LIKE THEY SAY...
YUCK!
IT COULDN'T HAVE HAPPENED TO A NICER GUY.

THE SURVIVING GERMANS RETREATED BACK TO THE EAST--RIGHT UNDER THE FIRE OF WATSON-COLE AND THE REST OF HIS MEN (AND WOMEN)!

DAS IST JA EINE SCHEISSE SITUATION!

BOY, ARE WE EVER GLAD TO BE BACK WITHIN OUR OWN LINES AGAIN!
CAPTAIN WATSON-COLE, WE HAVE NEW ORDERS FOR YOU.

WHAT IN THE WORLD DO THEY EXPECT OF US NOW!?
2ND ARMORED DIVISION IS SENDING A COLUMN OF TANKS BACK UP THROUGH THAT ROAD.

OUR ORDERS ARE TO SUPPORT THEM. AND SINCE YOU KNOW MORE ABOUT THAT LITTLE VALLEY THAN ANYBODY...
...YOU HAVE ORDERS TO GO WITH US.

I DON'T THINK THOSE ORDERS PERTAIN TO ALL OF US. THOSE OF YOU WHO WE PICKED UP ALONG THE WAY...
YOU CAN MAKE YOUR OWN CHOICE TO GO OR STAY.

I THINK I WILL STICK WITH YOU. BROADEN MY VIEW OF LIFE.

THAT IS...IF CANDELORA WILL STAY HERE AND LOOK AFTER MY MOTHER.
I WILL BE MORE THAN HAPPY TO DO THAT.

AND I WILL HELP HER.

I HOPE YOU'VE FINALLY DECIDED THAT I CAN BE TRUSTED. IF YOUR ANSWER IS YES...
I SHALL BE HAPPY TO FOLLOW YOU UP UP THAT ROAD, TO MESSINA, TO ROME, TO THE ALPS... WHEREVER IT TAKES ME.

WELL, I GUESS WE LEAVE YOU GIRLS HERE.

DO YOU THINK YOU WILL BE BACK THIS WAY SOMEDAY?
I DON'T KNOW.

BUT...I SURE WOULDN'T BE SURPRISED.
STRANGER THINGS HAVE HAPPENED.

WELL...IF YOU DO, TRY TO GIVE ME A LITTLE ADVANCE NOTICE.

GIVE ME TIME TO SHAVE MY LEGS!
HAHAHA!
THE END

CREATOR BIO

Since working on MARVEL's The 'Nam comic book series, Wayne Vansant has gone on to writing and illustrating numerous comics and graphics based on historical/military subjects. Titles such as DAYS OF DARKNESS, DAYS OF WRATH, NORMANDY, BOMBING NAZI GERMANY, GETTYSBURG, GRANT VS. LEE, THE BATTLE OF THE BULGE, KNIGHTS OF THE SKULL, KATUSKA, and an adaptation of Erich Maria Remaque's classic novel ALL QUIET ON THE WESTERN FRONT. Wayne has recently completed work on the 2nd and 3rd volumes of his World War II series BATTRON, about a French Legionnaire soldier's action/adventures during the war.

ALSO AVAILABLE FROM DON LOMAX

HIGH SHINING BRASS

High Shining Brass is based on the true story of an American spy during the Vietnam War as told to Don Lomax by agent Robert Durand who chronicles the tale. Durand was a member of a black-ops team, code- named "Shining Brass." The series depicts the horrific atrocities witnessed and performed by the once naïve special forces member as he attempts to perform his duties and understand the true meaning behind the madness. Durand's group was under the command of a combined force, comprised of every branch of the services, and headed up by the ever-popular Central Intelligence Committee. It's a journey into a shadow world of treachery and deceit—and reveals the way lives of Americans were traded about carelessly during the war in Vietnam.

ISBN: 978-1544962191 $14.99US

ABOVE AND BEYOND

Beginning in May of 2007, noted comic writer and illustrator Don Lomax teamed up with Police and Security News magazine to produce the series "Above and Beyond" - real life depictions of heroic acts by law enforcement professionals. Just as our soldiers here and abroad deserve recognition for their unwavering service, so do the men and women who protect and serve the citizens of the United States. Contained within these pages are just a few stories of these individuals who have demonstrated selfless bravery and heroic action under the most difficult circumstances and gone above and beyond the call of duty.

ISBN: 978-1635299601 $ 9.99 US

WWW.CALIBERCOMICS.COM

ALSO AVAILABLE FROM DON LOMAX

FIRE TEAM

Cam Ky MacMurphy is half-Vietnamese, half-American, and feels as if he doesn't belong to either race. His uncle, Nguyen Van Tan, raised him from birth and the two live in an area of town that is controlled by a skinhead gang. The neighborhood lives in fear as the gang forces them to pay "protection" money. Then hope appears in the form of a ghost from the past. When Nguyen was young he worked with a U.S. Fire Team deployed in the twilight days of the Vietnam War. The team ended up sacrificing their lives while trying to evacuate women and children from an overrun base. Now the Fire Team has come back from the dead to not only save Nguyen and Cam but bring news to Cam that his American father is alive and fighting a guerrilla war in the Vietnamese jungles!

ISBN: 978-1635297812 $16.99US

THE BOYS IN THE BASEMENT

For those that enjoy the world of model rail-roading! THE BOYS IN THE BASEMENT cartoon strip was conceived, written, and illustrated by award-winning comic book creator Don Lomax. Don made a career of working in the train industry before and after serving his country with a tour in Vietnam. Don takes a humorous look at the world of model trains from the perspective of three men, Merle and his friends Lenny and Earl, and their obsession and love with the hobby. As they attempt to build the perfect model railroad layout in Merle's basement.

ISBN: 978-1635298031 $ 12.99 US

WWW.CALIBERCOMICS.COM

DON'T MISS ANY OF MICHAEL KASNER'S HARD HITTING MILITARY NOVEL SERIES

BLACK OPS

Formed by an elite cadre of government officials, the Black OPS team goes where the law can't - to seek retribution for acts of terror directed against Americans anywhere in the world.

3 BOOK SERIES

Armed with all the tactical advantages of modern technology, battle hard and ready when the free world is threatened - the Peacekeepers are the baddest grunts on the planet.

4 BOOK SERIES

CHOPPER COPS

America is being torn apart as criminal cartels terrorize our cities, dealing drugs and death wholesale. Local police are outgunned, so the President unleashes the U.S. TACTICAL POLICE FORCE. An elite army of super cops with ammo to burn, they swoop down on the hot spots in sleek high-tech attack choppers to win the dirty war and take back America!

4 BOOK SERIES

FROM CALIBER BOOKS

www.calibercomics.com

DON'T MISS ANY OF NEIL HUNTER'S NOVELS FROM CALIBER BOOKS

Reporter Les Mason is completing an expose on the Long Point Nuclear Plant. But before he can finish he dies an agonizing death. The doctors are baffled—and there are similar cases to follow...Chris Lane, his girlfriend, and organizer of the Long Point Protestors, discovers Mason's notes, and decides to find out for herself what the plant has to hide.

2 BOOK SERIES

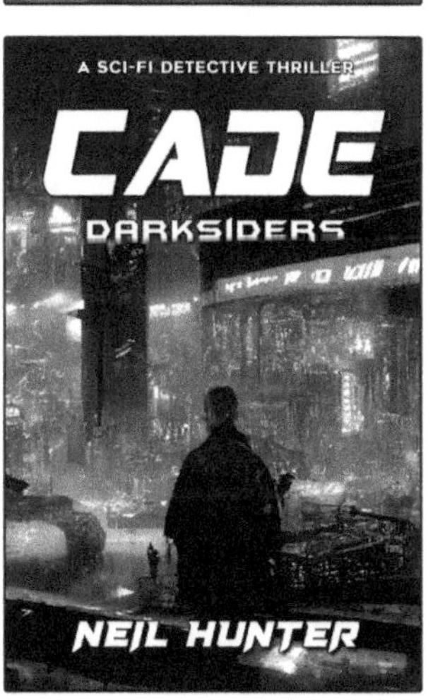

In middle of the 21st century America – over-populated decaying cities are ruled by hi-tech gangs pushing every vice and wastelands are controlled by bands of mutants. Ordinary citizens are oppressed and face a hopeless future. But Marshal T.J. Cade is a new breed of law enforcer. Teamed with his cyborg partner, Janek, Cade takes on these criminals and works in the gray areas of the law to get the job done.

3 BOOK SERIES

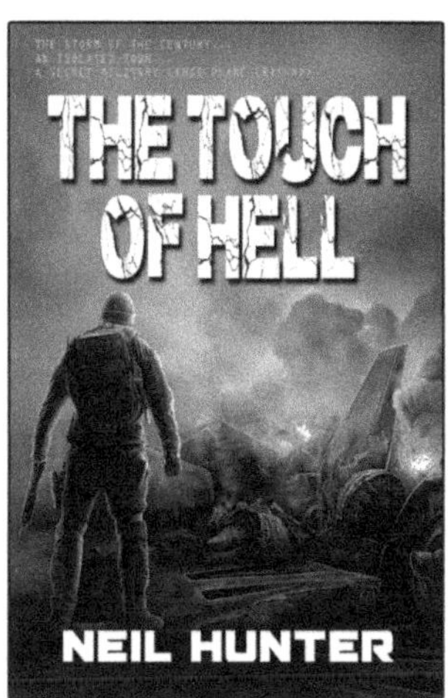

The village of Shepthorne England wasn't being gripped, but strangled by a winter's blanket of heavy snow and Arctic temperatures. The trouble began innocently enough with a massive pile-up of autos on frozen roads leading to and from the village. Then, from the sky, a military transport plane with its top secret cargo of devastation crashed down towards the center of the village. Hell was just beginning to touch Shepthorne and its unsuspecting citizens...

FROM CALIBER BOOKS

www.calibercomics.com

LOOKING FOR ACTION AND ADVENTURE
AUTHOR ALAN CAILLOU
NOVELS DELIVER!

AVAILABLE AT AMAZON.COM
FOR YOUR KINDLE OR IN PAPAERBACK
OR FROM
WWW.CALIBERCOMICS.COM

ALSO AVAILABLE FROM CALIBER COMICS

QUALITY GRAPHIC NOVELS TO ENTERTAIN

THE SEARCHERS: VOLUME 1
The Shape of Things to Come

Before *League of Extraordinary Gentlemen* there was *The Searchers*. At the dawn of the 20th Century the greatest literary adventurers from the minds of Wells, Doyle, Burroughs, and Haggard were created. All thought to be the work of pure fiction. However, a century later, the real-life descendents of those famous characters are recuited by the legendary Professor Challenger in order to save mankind's future. Series collected for the first time.

"Searchers is the comic book I have on the wall with a sign reading - 'Love books? Never read a comic? Try this one! ....money back guarantee..." - Dark Star Books.

WAR OF THE WORLDS: INFESTATION

Based on the H.G. Wells classic! The "Martian Invasion" has begun again and now mankind must fight for its very humanity. It happened slowly at first but by the third year, it seemed that the war was almost over... the war was almost lost.

"Writer Randy Zimmerman has a fine grasp of drama, and spins the various strands of the story into a coherent whole... imaginative and very gritty."
- war-of-the-worlds.co.uk

HELSING: LEGACY BORN

From writer Gary Reed (Deadworld) and artists John Lowe (Captain America), Bruce McCorkindale (Godzilla). She was born into a legacy she wanted no part of and pushed into a battle recessed deep in the shadows of the night. Samantha Helsing is torn between two worlds...two allegiances...two families. The legacy of the Van Helsing family and their crusade against the "night creatures" comes to modern day with the most unlikely of all warriors.

"Congratulations on this masterpiece..."
- Paul Dale Roberts, Compuserve Reviews

DEADWORLD

Before there was The Walking Dead there was Deadworld. Here is an introduction of the long running classic horror series, Deadworld, to a new audience! Considered by many to be the godfather of the original zombie comic with over 100 issues and graphic novels in print and over 1,000,000 copies sold, Deadworld ripped into the undead with intelligent zombies on a mission and a group of poor teens riding in a school bus desperately try to stay one step ahead of the sadistic, Harley-riding King Zombie. Death, mayhem, and a touch of supernatural evil made Deadworld a classic and now here's your chance to get into the story!

DAYS OF WRATH

Award winning comic writer & artist Wayne Vansant brings his gripping World War II saga of war in the Pacific to Guadalcanal and the Battle of Bloody Ridge. This is the powerful story of the long, vicious battle for Guadalcanal that occurred in 1942-43. When the U.S. Navy orders its outnumbered and out-gunned ships to run from the Japanese fleet, they abandon American troops on a bloody, battered island in the South Pacific.

"Heavy on authenticity, compellingly written and beautifully drawn."
- Comics Buyers Guide

SHERLOCK HOLMES:
THE CASE OF THE MISSING MARTIAN

Sherlock is called out of retirement to London in 1908 to solve a most baffling mystery: The British Museum is missing a specimen of a Martian from the failed invasion of 1899. Did it walk away on its own or did someone steal it?

Holmes ponders the facts and remembers his part in the war effort alongside Professor Challenger during the War of the Worlds invasion that was chronicled in H.G. Wells' classic novel.

Meanwhile, Doctor Watson has problems of his own when his wife steals a scalpel from his surgical tool kit and returns to her old stomping grounds of Whitechapel, the London

CALIBER PRESENTS

The original Caliber Presents anthology title was one of Caliber's inaugural releases and featured predominantly new creators, many of which went onto successful careers in the comics' industry. In this new version, Caliber Presents has expanded to graphic novel size and while still featuring new creators it also includes many established professional creators with new visions. Creators featured in this first issue include nominees and winners of some of the industry's major awards including the Eisner, Harvey, Xeric, Ghastly, Shel Dorf, Comic Monsters, and more.

LEGENDLORE

From Caliber Comics now comes the entire Realm and Legendlore saga as a set of volumes that collects the long running critically acclaimed series. In the vein of The Lord of The Rings and The Hobbit with elements of Game of Thrones and Dungeon and Dragons.

Four normal modern day teenagers are plunged into a world they thought only existed in novels and film. They are whisked away to a magical land where dragons roam the skies, orcs and hobgoblins terrorize travelers, where unicorns prance through the forest, and kingdoms wage war for dominance. It is a world where man is just one race, joining other races such as elves, trolls, dwarves, changelings, and the dreaded night creatures who steal the night.

TIME GRUNTS

What if Hitler's last great Super Weapon was – Time itself! A WWII/time travel adventure that can best be described as *Band of Brothers* meets *Time Bandits*.

October, 1944. Nazi fortunes appear bleaker by the day. But in the bowels of the Wenceslas Mines, a terrible threat has emerged . . . The Nazis have discovered the ability to conquer time itself with the help of a new ominous device!

Now a rag tag group of American GIs must stop this threat to the past, present, and future . . . While dealing with their own past, prejudices, and fears in the process.

CALIBER
C O M I C S

www.calibercomics.com

www.ingramcontent.com/pod-product-compliance
Lightning Source LLC
Chambersburg PA
CBHW041158100726
47911CB00016B/785